After All This Time

J.M. GOODRICH

J.M. Goodrich is a native of Michigan's beautiful upper peninsula. She loves spending time outdoors as much as she can with her family when she's not reading or writing. She has been published in several different anthologies and novels of her own. She has written stories of romance, fantasy, and horror. In addition to her love of writing, she has a passion for music, and an obsession with The Beatles.

Also By J.M. Goodrich

Deadly Celebrations

Emily's Wish

Snowflakes & Heartaches

Undying Love

Coming Home

Love Me Right

Summer Nights

Spirit And Soul

Bruised Heart

Just One Night

One

I SAT WATCHING the steam rise and curl off my cup of coffee, until it disappeared into nothing. I concentrated on nothing else as it bobbed and weaved its way through the air, hoping it would take my mind off of Eric.

Eric was my best friend. We have pretty much been inseparable since we were kids. It's always been just the two of us, for as long as I could remember. He's always been the one I'd run to first with any news that I might have had. Good or bad. He was always the one I wanted to spend all my time with.

He's gone from helping to fix my skinned knees to helping mend my broken heart.

At first everything was normal. My feelings towards Eric were merely those of friendship, contentment, comfort. But as we got older they developed into something deeper. And it wasn't long before I realized I was in love with him.

But I could never do anything about it. Eric had never shown any interest in me romantically, at least not that I could see. And he was popular, always the center of attention, loved by everyone and always surrounded by people, especially women.

I didn't stand a chance.

Besides, he always seemed to be in a relationship. I swear, it was like the man was allergic to being single. So even if I wanted to, there really never was an opportunity for me to tell him how I felt.

I, on the other hand, was the complete opposite. Not that I was like, super shy or anything like that. I suppose on some level I avoided relationships with other men. All the while secretly hoping that Eric would suddenly wake up one day and realize that he had feelings for me.

Pathetic, I know. But right now, hope was all I had.

For weeks now I've been trying to pull myself together, gather the courage to tell my best friend that I've been in love with him all this time.

Today I was finally going to tell him.

I let out a slow, deep breath, trying to calm my nerves. My entire body felt tense. I had no idea how

Eric was going to react. Would he say he had feelings for me as well? Would he be mad? Would he laugh at me? I really hoped he at least wouldn't laugh at me. I think I would be both humiliated and broken-hearted if he did.

And would this shatter our lifelong friendship?

Shit.

Now I was beginning to lose the small amount of confidence I had managed to work up. Closing my eyes, I took in another slow breath. I have to do this. I've put it off way too many times before. I've waited long enough.

The little bell above the front door rang out, announcing the presence of a new customer. My eyes flew open, following the sound. Panic began to creep up inside me. Usually, I ignored the sound of the bell, this was a pretty popular little coffee shop, people were constantly going in and out. But today was different. Today I seemed to notice every little noise around me, every scent, every small little detail that would just normally pass me by, unnoticed.

And it had me on edge.

My breath hitched as I caught sight of Eric. His tall, muscular build filled out most of the door frame. His dark brown hair was messy, sticking out a little here and there. From here it looked to be a bit damp still, like he had come here straight from the shower. The thought of him like that made me blush.

But I'd be lying if I said I hadn't had at least a few thoughts of him like that over the years.

Eric smiled as he noticed me, and headed straight for the counter to place his order. We both had the same thing every time we came here. Always ordered the caramel flavored coffee. Sometimes I would have a scone or donut to go with it, but I was too nervous to even think about food right now. My stomach was in knots.

After grabbing his drink, Eric made his way over to me. "Morning, sunshine," he said as he slid into the booth of our favorite table.

And just like that, every ounce of confidence I had evaporated, like the steam off my coffee. Just one look into his piercing blue eyes and I forget the speech I had practiced all week in front of my mirror. All I could do now was smile and nod my head like an idiot.

I felt defeated.

A coward.

My feelings for him are almost overwhelming. I can't ignore them much longer. He has to know how I feel. But how? When?

I hated this.

"You got any big plans for tonight?" Eric asked me.

I shook my head. "Just the usual - go to work, come home and clean my apartment, and maybe start reading a new book." So exciting, I know. "What about you?"

Eric took a sip of his coffee. "I thought I'd check out that party they're having tonight. The one at the old warehouse."

'They' probably meant his old football buddies from college. They all still hung out all the time, causing a lot of trouble, hitting on any woman they could. Which was just about any that could walk and talk and was over the age of eighteen. Not exactly what I would call good company.

"You wanna come with me?" Eric asked, knowing full well that it was not my kind of scene. "It could be fun. You need to do something different, shake up your routine every once in a while."

" I don't know," I gripped my coffee cup for comfort. "You know I don't do well at parties." I think the last one I actually attended was back right before our high school graduation. Everyone was completely wasted. I had several drinks accidentally spilled on me, ruining the dress I had bought specifically to try and impress Eric with. And some time during that night I had lost sight of him and ended up spending the rest of the night by myself.

Rumors that night were he found himself a nice quiet spot to be alone with the captain of the cheerleading squad.

I've actively avoided any party since then.

Eric batted his eyelashes at me, making me laugh. "Please, Jess. If you come, I promise not to leave your side the entire night."

"Just like graduation, huh?" I mumbled.

"Huh?"

I shook my head quickly. "Nothing. But why is it so important that I come with you?"

"It's important," he said, biting into the massive breakfast sandwich he had ordered, "because you're my best friend. I like hanging out with you," he answered simply, taking another bite.

I felt the heat creeping up the back of my neck.

"Besides," he continued, "you've been so dang busy lately. You need to get out of the house, let off some steam. Hang out with your best friend in the entire world. So what do you say? I need my best girl by my side."

I rolled my eyes at him. "Well, when you put it that way, how could I refuse?" I laughed.

Eric quickly shoved the last of his sandwich into his mouth, wiping the crumbs off his hands and onto his pants. I don't think I've ever seen the man use a napkin, even though there was a pile of them sitting right in front of him. "I'll take that as a yes," he replied. "I'll meet you there around ten tonight. Sound good?"

I nodded, even though it didn't. The spending time with Eric part did. The party - not so much.

"Sweet." He checked his watch. "I know I just got here, but I gotta head into work a little early. We're putting in some extra roadways just north or town." Eric worked in construction. He practically did it all - roads, houses, even a little plumbing. He didn't mind getting dirty. Plus, all that hard work resulted in a rock hard body that I, and every other female, like to appreciate. Secretly, of course, on my end. "So I'll catch ya later," he said. He threw me a wink before heading out of the coffee shop.

I slumped back in the booth, letting out the breath I hadn't known I'd been holding. I felt so stupid letting this opportunity pass me by. Again. I really should have just told Eric how I felt. Now I had to go to some stupid party I didn't want to go to with people I didn't even like.

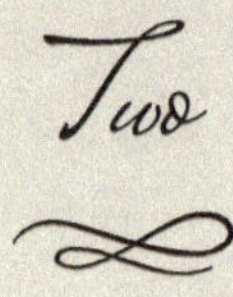

Two

"SO . . . WHAT DID HE SAY?" Stacy asked anxiously. "Did he confess his love for you? Are you two going to ride off into the sunset together? Can I help plan the wedding?"

"Whoa there," I laughed. "You gotta slow down."

"But why? You've been waiting for like, forever for this moment. I'm excited for you."

"Well, you're excited over nothing," I all but whispered.

"What did you say?"

'Nothing," I sighed deeply. "I actually never got the chance to tell him."

"What?! Why not? You didn't wimp out on me, did you?" I swear I could hear her eyes rolling in her head. To be fair, I know how many times I have told her 'tonight's the night. I'm gonna tell him.' I lost count.

"No, I didn't wimp out. I was going to, I swear. But then Eric brought up this party tonight and asked me to go. I lost all confidence. So see, it wasn't my fault, really," I laughed awkwardly. "But you're coming with me, right?"

"Of course," Stacy said. "I'll come over after work and we can get ready together."

"I don't think I can do this, Stace," I cried. "Maybe we're just destined to be friends. Nothing more. I mean, if it was going to happen between us, wouldn't it have already happened by now? I don't know how much longer I can do this," I whispered that last part. I had already held on for so long, held on to so much hope. I don't think I had it in me to do it much longer.

"Yes, you can," my best friend reassures me.

"I don't know. I feel sick. This whole thing makes me feel sick," I admitted.

Stacy sat me down and took a seat beside me. "It's just nerves, Jess. That's why you feel sick. You can do this, I promise. You're totally overthinking things and worrying too much. You've gotta get out of your own head, girl. You got yourself all worked up. Just breathe," she told me.

I wanted to believe Stacy. I really did. But what if she was wrong?

Closing my eyes, I took in a deep breath, slowly letting it out. I did this over and over, until I could feel myself calming down.

"Are you good now?" Stace asked, her voice gentle.

"I think so."

Her smile widened. "Good. Now let's finish getting you ready so we can walk into that party and you can tell your other best friend," she winked at me, " how you feel about him and then you two can fall madly in love and live happily ever after."

Stacy and I arrived at the old warehouse where the party was being held. I had never been to one of these before. It just wasn't my scene. Stacy, on the other hand, would occasionally go out on the weekend and party. She would constantly try to drag me along with her but I would always refuse.

There weren't too many people here so it wasn't too terribly uncomfortable. Yet. The night was still young.

I scan the room, spotting Eric at one of the

makeshift bars in the back. He was sitting there, by himself. Stacy spotted him too, and she grabbed my hand and led me through the small crowd on the dancefloor to him. "Hey Eric," she said as she plopped herself down on a barstool. She left one open between Eric and herself. She gestured for me to take the open one.

"Hey! You made it," he said, throwing himself on me for a hug. I wanted to hug him back so badly, but my body didn't react. This was the first time I can ever remember Eric hugging me.

"It was hard work convincing her to come," Stacy told him.

"Well, I appreciate that you did."

The barstools were so close together that Eric's leg would occasionally bump into mine, or his arms would brush mine whenever he grabbed his beer to take a sip. Every little touch sent little electric shocks throughout my entire body. It was all I could concentrate on.

I almost fell off my stool as Stacy dragged me to the dance floor. She motioned for Eric to join us too but he smiled and shook his head, pointing to the full beer in his hand. So the two of us hit the dance floor for a bit.

"Are you having fun?" She leaned in and asked. The music was so loud and there were so many people that you had to be really close in order to hear the person talking to you.

"I am," I said, meaning it. I haven't had this much fun in a long time. We danced and twirled to the music, having the time of our lives. Between the music and the laughter, the drinks and the company, I was finally feeling ready to tell Eric everything.

"I think I'm ready!" I yell to Stace over the music.

She gives me a puzzled look. "Ready for what?"

"To tell him."

She stopped dancing and stared at me, wide eyed. "Seriously?"

"Seriously," I nodded. I don't know what exactly it was, but I felt ready to walk over to Eric, look him in the eyes, and tell him that I have been in love with him for years. And I still am. I have never loved anyone like this before. He was not only my best friend. He was so much more. He was everything to me.

She twirled me around to face the bar, where Eric was still seated. Putting her hands on my shoulders, she told me, "You go to him. Tell him everything that's in your heart. Now," she gives me a push in his direction, "go get your man."

I gathered up all my courage and walked up to the bar, keeping my head held high. I would *not* lose it this time. I would walk out of this place tonight having told him, whether he accepted my love or just wanted to remain friends. Either way, Eric would know how I felt about him.

As I got closer to the bar, Eric suddenly turned around. He noticed me and smiled wide. God, he was sexy.

"About time," he said, standing up off his stool. Did he already know how I felt about him? Stacy must have spoken to him while I was in the bathroom earlier. I breathed a sigh of relief. If that was the case, then it would make this a little easier for me.

As I opened my mouth to say something a female voice sounded out from behind me, calling out Eric's name. I watched as she ran and jumped into his arms. He caught her and she giggled, kissing him full on the mouth.

My heart instantly shattered.

The music died down and everyone and everything around me blurred together. I couldn't concentrate on anything but the sight in front of me.

He was dating someone. Eric's heart belonged to someone else. And I was about to make a fool out of myself. How could I not have known? Why hadn't he said anything? I didn't even know he was even talking to other girls. I couldn't believe it. I didn't want to believe it.

I ran through the crowd, right past Stacy, tears streaming down my face. I could hear her calling my name, but I don't stop. I can't face her, I can't face anyone right now. How could I be so stupid?

I ran to Stacy's car and hopped in. I closed the door, completely breaking down. Stacy slid into the driver's seat. "What the hell happened?" She asked.

"You didn't see?" I asked between sobs. She shook her head.

"Eric had a girlfriend."

"Eric had a girl already? When did that happen?"

I shook my head, looking down at the floor. I had no idea. I had seen him just this morning, at the coffee shop. He didn't say a word. Didn't even hint at it.

"Oh, sweetie," she rubbed my shoulder. "I am so sorry. If I knew I would have told you. And I certainly wouldn't have sent you over there. Is there anything I can do? Do you want me to go beat her up? Because I will. You know I will."

I couldn't laugh. I couldn't do anything but cry, feeling completely broken. "I just want to go home," I whispered. So she drove me home.

I wasn't in the mood to talk, even to Stacy, so I asked her to just drop me off and head home herself. She was hesitant to leave me alone, but ultimately agreed. She's always been the one to make me feel better, the one I cried to whenever something went wrong. She was basically my go-to person in life.

But right now I just couldn't do it. I couldn't hold up a conversation. I didn't want to be comforted. I didn't want to be told that everything would be alright. I know it will be, eventually.

But right now, it wasn't. And I wanted to be alone.

I opened my front door and turned to quickly wave at Stacy, letting her know it was okay to leave. I close and lock the door, not bothering to turn on any lights. A dark house to match my mood.

As I stood there in the dark, wondering how everything could have gone so wrong, I suddenly heard Eric call out my name. At first I thought that I was just hearing things, but then the knocking on my front door began.

"Jess!" Eric yelled. "Jess, are you in there? What's going on? Jess!"

His voice was filled with worry, concern. It somehow broke my heart a little more. Tears slid down my face as I crouched on the opposite side of the door, hidden in the shadows, my heart breaking more with each thump of his fist.

Three

I DID NOT WANT to get out of bed this morning. I wanted to stay here snuggled up in my blankets all day. They were warm, they were safe.

They wouldn't break my heart.

I checked my phone and saw that I had several missed calls and texts. A couple were from Stace, asking me to get ahold of her when I woke up, and the rest were all from Eric. I tossed the phone at the end of the bed, not bothering to read a single message.

I drifted back to sleep for a few hours and was woken up by the sound of someone walking around in my house. I was about to reach for my phone to call the police when my best friend peeked her head inside my bedroom door.

"About time you got up, sleepyhead."

"Thanks for the heart attack," I said, grabbing my chest. "You just about scared the shit out of me."

Stacy just laughed.

"How'd you get in anyway?" I asked as she moved the blankets to uncover me. I thought I locked the door.

"You gave me a key for emergencies," she shrugged. "Now, come on. I ordered up a pizza and it'll be here any minute. So get your ass dressed."

I grumbled but did as I was told, getting up and putting clothes on. Really, all I did was throw on a different pair of pajamas. My daytime pj's, if you will. I was dressing for comfort, not to impress.

I gathered the plates, napkins, and drinks while Stacy answered the door for the pizza delivery. "So," she said, taking a huge bite, "spill, girl. What happened yesterday?"

I really didn't wanna talk about it yet. But I knew she wasn't going to let it go. I took in a deep breath, letting it out slowly. "Everything went wrong," I shook my head. "I was ready. Finally ready to tell Eric that I was in love with him. And then . . . *she* happened," I said, sounding disgusted. I picked at my food. I wasn't hungry all of a sudden. "Did you know?"

She shook her head, eyes wide. "I didn't. I swear. You know I wouldn't hold that information from you if I did. And I certainly wouldn't have convinced you to go talk to him. He never said anything to you? Not even a hint that he was dating someone?"

"Not a word."

"That's messed up. I'm sorry."

I shrugged my shoulders, not knowing what else to say.

"So how do you feel?"

"Honestly, I have no idea," I admitted. "I mean, I know I'm hurt and brokenhearted and about a million other things right now. But other than that . . ."

"You should talk to him."

I shot her a look. "Seriously?"

She shrugged. "Yeah, why not?"

Because he just tore my heart out and stomped on it? Because I'm not ready?

Because I don't want to?

"I wouldn't even know what to say to him." I just want to pretend this never happened. Is that a thing? Could I do that? "What if this completely ruins our friendship? He's been my best friend forever."

Stacy cleared her throat, giving me the side-eye.

"Besides you," I offered her a weak laugh. "I just don't think I could handle it if he wasn't in my life anymore."

"I get that," she said as scooted over to my side of

the couch. She put her arm around me and I laid my head down on her shoulder. "But you two have been through so much together. He deserves to know what's going on. And so do you. That's a talk only the two of you can have. No one else."

I knew she was right. And I hated that she was. Knowing that this was unavoidable didn't make it any easier. It wasn't going to make my heart break any less. If anything, it was only going to break more.

"I've been in love with him for most of my life," I sighed heavily.

"I know," she said, hugging me close. "I know."

Four

I WAS SITTING out on my front porch the
evening after Stacy left. She had stayed for a few hours,
trying to cheer me up. Then she said she had some
urgent business and took off, which didn't bother me
since I preferred to be alone right now. She was a good
friend, she really was. I was going to need time though.
A lot of time before I could start to feel somewhat
normal again.

I had seen Eric in relationships before. That wasn't
the issue. What was the issue was the fact that this time
I was ready to tell him how I felt. Before, I knew I
wasn't ready. So him being in a relationship bothered
me, sure. But not nearly as much as it did now. Not
when I had been minutes away from telling him what

was inside my heart. I felt humiliated even though I had never said a word

I was taking a sip of my tea when I saw his truck pull up. I almost choked on it. Holy shit, I was not ready for this. He parked and hopped out, walking towards me. He didn't look angry, which was a good sign. I pulled the blanket on my lap closer to me, wishing I could hide under it and avoid this conversation entirely.

"Can we talk?" He asked.

I nodded, without saying a word, and Eric took a seat on the rocking chair to my right. This had been my grandparents house before I inherited it. And sitting out here together each evening, drinking tea and watching the stars was one of their evening routines. Sitting out here doing the same thing made me feel close to them. I really missed them both.

"Stacy came to talk to me," he began. "She filled me in on everything that's been going on."

I shifted uncomfortably in my seat. How could she do this to me? She knew I wasn't ready to talk about this with him yet. And it was something that I really needed to talk to him about myself, not through her or anyone else.

"Please don't be mad at her, she's just worried about you."

Still . . .

"I'm sorry I didn't tell you about her sooner. I should have."

"Why didn't you?" I ask, finding my voice.

Eric sat back in the rocking chair. "At first I didn't think what was going on between us was anything serious. I don't have those kinds of relationships. Girls usually don't stick around," he shrugged like it was no big deal. But it was. It was a huge deal to me, even if he didn't know it. He also didn't know that unlike any of these other girls, I would have stuck around. To the very end.

"But then she didn't go anywhere. And she started calling me her boyfriend. And I liked it."

And just like that, my heart fractured a little more.

"I would really like it if you could find a way to be happy for me. You and I have been through too much to lose our friendship over this. You mean too much to me." Hearing him say those words was like a punch to the gut. He meant a lot to me too. I guess we just meant different things to each other. He meant a whole lot more to me than I did to him. His tone of voice made it sound like friends were all that we would ever be.

"But she means a lot to me too," he continued,

"Her name is Julie, and I think the two of you would get along."

"I would love for you to meet her," he tried again when I hadn't said anything.

"I don't know," I shook my head. "I'm not sure if that's a good idea."

"Why not?" Eric looked confused. "My best friend and my girlfriend should at least meet each other at least once."

Girlfriend. Hearing him say that word destroyed me. I wanted to be the one he called his girlfriend.

"I don't know . . ."

"Please, Jess," he begged. "It would mean a lot to me."

Damn it.

"Fine," I huffed. But I wasn't going to like it. I wasn't going to like her.

Five

I WAS SEATED DIRECTLY across from Eric's girlfriend, Julie. I even hated her name. Eric sat right next to her. From the second I sat down she started gushing about Eric and how perfect he was. How amazing and attentive and sexy he was.

Nothing that was new to me.

She may have been nervous and rambling on and on, but to me it kind of felt like she was maybe marking her territory. Women usually did that when they found out that their man's best friend was a girl.

But overall she seemed genuinely nice and really into Eric. In fact, they both seemed super into each other. As much as I hated to admit it, they did seem good together. And happy. So I agreed to suck it up and try to get along with her, for Eric's sake. No matter how much it tore my heart apart to see them together.

We were on our way out when Julie stopped and grabbed me by the arm. "I have a great idea," she said, smiling from ear to ear. "How about me and you continue to get to know each other. Without this guy here," she nodded towards Eric.

He pretended to look offended. "Are you sick of me already?" he asked her.

She threw him a wink. "Of course." She let go of me, jumping up to give him a quick kiss. "You know I never will. I just thought we could use some girl time."

"I think it's a great idea. Jess? What do you say?"

I say it's a terrible idea and I just want to go home. I looked at my car. I was so close to an escape. But I didn't want to disappoint Eric in any way. "I guess," I put on my best fake smile. "I can ask Stacy to meet up with us too," I suggested. "She's my other best friend." Her being there would be a huge help. I didn't want to be alone with this girl.

"Awesome," Julie said, in a tone that was a little too cheerful for me. I groaned inwardly and called up Stacy. She was all too eager to come help me 'spy' on the new girl, as she put it. "You better not forget about me," Stacy jokes.

"What do you mean?"

"You know, when you and Julie become best friends," she laughed.

"I seriously doubt you have anything to worry about."

"Yeah, well, that's why I agreed to go. I need to make sure no one steals my best friend." I rolled my eyes at her through the phone. There was no way that was going to happen.

Julie insisted that we go hang out at the mall. There was a ton to do there and also she wanted help picking out some clothes for future dates with Eric. It was absolute torture for me. Who in their right mind would want to help some girl pick out clothes so she could look good for the guy you were secretly in love with?

I was kicking myself for not speaking up sooner. If I had not been so damn scared I would be anywhere but here, happy and content with the love of my life.

But no, I had to be scared and afraid, so here I was, trailing along behind my best friend, linked arm-in-arm with another girl as they excitedly talked about boys and clothes and whatever else was on their minds.

The worst part was that Julie was actually pretty great. But I couldn't allow myself to admit that. I wanted to hate her. I needed to hate her. It made me feel better about the whole situation. The situation that I created.

I would give anything to be able to fix it.

After a couple hours of wandering around the mall I was more than ready to call it quits. I hated malls in the first place. But Julie and Stacy had barely just begun. So I offered to just head home myself and they could continue on their little adventure. Stacy was a little too excited about that idea for my liking. She was supposed to be my best friend, not Julie's. So reluctantly, I said my goodbye's and left them to continue shopping.

Stacy called me later that night to brag all about Julie and how amazing she was. They even made plans to hang out that weekend, just the two of them. "Oh," she said after a minute, "I mean, you could come too if you wanted."

Thanks for the pity invite. "No, that's okay," I told her. You two enjoy your little friendship.

"Are you sure?"

"Absolutely."

"You're such a great friend. Gotta go, talk to you later," she said before hanging up. Usually when she called we would talk for hours and she would end up stopping by to talk more and gossip in person. I couldn't help but feel a little hurt at all this. I didn't think I would lose both the man I love and my best friend to this woman. It stung like hell.

Six

IT'S BEEN about a week and I haven't heard from anyone. Not a single word from Eric, Stacy, or even Julie. I've tried calling, texting-nothing. It raised my anxiety levels up to an eleven. I had no idea what the hell was going on, or if everyone was okay. And if they were okay, why was everyone ignoring me?

I went over the last time we were together many times in my mind. I can't think of anything I might have said or done that would have caused everyone important in my life to just ghost me like this. I was nothing but pleasant to everyone.

Wasn't I?

I know I didn't exactly welcome Julie into my life with welcoming, open arms. But I wasn't rude or hateful or anything.

This was all driving me nuts.

I sat in the coffee shop, like I have every morning, waiting to see if Eric would stop by. He hadn't been here in over a week, according to the girls who worked here. Since Eric and I used to come here together daily, they knew us pretty well. But even they hadn't seen him in a while. I was really beginning to worry. It was one thing to stop calling me or even come by the house. But it was another thing to just stop doing something that had been our daily routine now for years.

What did I do that was so wrong? And how could I have not seen it while it was happening?

I was just about to give up and go home when Eric stumbled through the door. He looked rough. His hair was messy and sticking up everywhere, but not in that sexy, just-woke-up kinda way. You could tell he hadn't shaved in a few days either by the stubble on his face, and the dark circles under eyes completed his new look. I've never seen him like this before. He usually looked at least somewhat put together. Never like this. It was alarming. He took one quick look at me and walked over to the counter to grab a coffee.

Silently he slid into the booth across from me, taking a long sip from his extra large coffee.

"You're looking well," I teased.

Eric shook his head. "It's been one hell of a week, let me tell you."

I waited for him to elaborate.

"I've missed you," I told him, my voice small.

"I am so sorry I have been MIA," he stared down at the table. "Trust me though, there was a good reason."

"Well it better be damn good," I said, a little anger leaking out in my voice. "We've been friends for a very long time. And you've never treated me like this." I didn't mean to snap at him, but I've never been this angry at him either.

Eric winced. "I deserve that I suppose." Damn right. "Let me finish this," he gestured to his cup, "and then I'll tell you everything."

We finished our coffees and went for a walk as we talked. Eric said he needed to keep moving, which only made me feel even more worried. We found a trail that led down to the river, walking a few minutes in silence. Finally, Eric took a deep breath before he spoke.

"I really want to apologize. For everything," he began. "I didn't tell you about Julie at first because none of my relationships ever last long. You know that."

It was true. Usually by the time he told me there were already fizzling out and he was ready to move on.

"But my relationship with Julie was different. I wanted her around for a long time. I loved being with her."

My heart twisted hearing those words from him. But I stayed silent, letting him talk.

"That night that we met at the warehouse party was when I had planned for you two to meet and to tell you that I was in a relationship with her. But that didn't go as planned."

"I'm sorry," I said. "That was kinda my fault."

He turned to face me. "What *did* happen that night?"

"I . . ." I debated on whether or not to tell him. He was happy and in a relationship, and I didn't want to ruin that. But then I remembered we were in this whole mess because I decided to keep my mouth shut in the first place. If I would have just sucked it up and told him from the beginning, nine of this would be happening right now. This would all be a different story.

"I panicked," I said at last. It was now or never. "I had gone there that night with the intention of telling you how I feel."

"And how is that?"

My heart was hammering out of my chest. "I am in

love with you, Eric. I have been for many years now," I said quickly before I lost my nerve.

I looked over at Eric, who hadn't said anything in response. I couldn't read the expression on his face, so I had no idea how he felt. So I continued. "I didn't say anything because I didn't know how you would react and I didn't want to lose what we have now, our friendship. And I was scared," I added quietly.

Eric nodded, just seeming to take in everything.

"I'm sorry to bring this up now," I said, "with you being so happy with Julie and all. You know I've always had shitty timing," I said with a weak laugh, trying to lighten the mood.

"Actually, I'm not," he said, breaking his silence. "Julie and I are no longer together."

Well, that was news. "I'm so sorry to hear that."

"Wait til you hear why," he said with a hint of amusement in his voice. "I hadn't heard much from her all week. Which was really confusing considering how well we were getting along. I thought our relationship was going places. But she stopped coming by and calling me," like I did to you," he added, looking apologetic. "And then one day I heard a knock at the door. I raced to open it, thinking it was Julie, only to find Stacy standing there."

"Stacy?" I was totally confused.

"Yup," he nodded. "She told me that we needed to talk. So long story short . . . The more she and Julie hung out, the closer they got. They felt closer than just friends. Neither of them had experienced feelings like this before and well, they decided to explore these feelings."

I'm not sure if I knew where this story was going.

"While exploring these feelings," he said, sounding almost as confused as I was, " they found out that they might really be into each other."

Nope, I didn't know where that story was going. At all.

I stopped in my tracks. "Wait-what? Stacy is . . . into women?" Not that it would be a bad thing. I fully support love in any form it came in. I was just surprised. I have known Stacy all my life. She had never even hinted that she might be into women at all.

"I was shocked too," Eric said. "I've never had a girlfriend leave me for another woman before," he laughed.

"I wonder why she never said anything to me? We usually talk about everything."

"She didn't want to hurt you," he told me. "She also said that Julie wanted me to know that she was leaving me and that she and Stacy were going to officially give it a try, as a couple. And that they really didn't know how to tell either one of us."

Holy shit. This was a lot to take in.

We walked down to the river and sat in the sand along the water.

"Stacy also told me a little more about your feelings for me," he said.

She what? How could she do that? "What? Why? That's something that I should have told you myself." A long time ago.

"Again, she said it was because she didn't want to see you hurt. She said that you were a mess when Julie and I got together. I'm sorry I didn't see it."

"You didn't know. It's okay," I shrugged.

He shifted to face me, bringing his hand up to tilt my chin so I was looking at him. "But it's not okay. I hurt you, and that's the last thing I'd ever want to do. You've been the only one there for me, always. You're the one true constant thing in my life. And I never want to lose you."

My heart was beating wildly in my chest. I had longed to hear this sort of thing from him.

"I never want to lose you, either," I told him. "That's why I didn't tell you how I felt. I was scared and didn't want to lose you ever as a friend. If that's all we'll ever be, then I'll take it. I want you in my life. I need you." I breathed.

"After I processed all the information that Stacy had told me, I sat down and actually thought about us. You and I," he added.

Here it comes, I thought. The dreaded 'we'll always be friends' talk. And then things between us will be awkward for a while. And we'll eventually just stop talking altogether when it becomes too much. And then I'll lose the only person that ever really mattered to me.

Eric looked me in the eyes. "After thinking things over, *really* thinking things over," he said, "I think I might be in love with you too."

My heart stopped beating and my breath hitched. Did he just say what I think he said?

"It's always been you," he continued. "You're the one there for me, no matter what. You're the one I lean on when I need someone. You're the only thing on my mind day and night. At first I thought it was because of how close our friendship is. But then I realized that it's more than that. So much more. I want you in my life. I can't imagine my life without you in it. And I don't want to. I want you to be mine."

"You do?" I breathed. This had to be a dream. There was no way I was this lucky. But then Eric's mouth was on mine, and all thoughts were abandoned. I gave in and melted into his arms, kissing him back.

This was everything that I ever wanted.

Eric pulled back, looking at me with love in his eyes for the first time. "I can't believe it was you, after all this time."

www.ingramcontent.com/pod-product-compliance
Lightning Source LLC
Chambersburg PA
CBHW031453310726
48971CB00003B/898

I've been in love with my best friend for years, I've just never found the right time to tell him.

But just when I've gathered the courage to tell him, I'm blindsided with the news that he's in love with another woman.

I'm too late.

This time it looks serious, and I fear I've lost the chance to tell him how I feel.

This wasn't how it was supposed to go. He was supposed to be mine.

This can't be how our story ends.

J.M. Goodrich